A BEAR HUG

at Bedtime

Jana
Novotny Hunter

illustrated by
Kay Widdowson

In my jungle, there's a TIGER.
She's a **stripy**, orange tiger...

...hiding behind trees,
chasing me through
tall grasses —
ready to **pounce!**

I *run, run, run,*
over, under and through.

BUT...

...if she's *quick* and catches up,
as tigers often can...

...I stroke her fur and snuggle
up to my stripy Tiger Gran.

In my forest,
there's a MONKEY.

She's a **mischief-maker**
monkey...

...leaping
through tall branches,
dangling by her tail —
ready to spring!

We
swing, swing, swing,

high above the trees.

BUT...

...if she **jumps** down to the ground,
the minute that she lands...

...we'll **roll around** like acrobats

and balance on our hands.

In my desert, there's a LIZARD.

He's a **cheeky**, sneaky lizard,
crawling towards me, ready to dart.

We **dig, dig, dig,**
and make a massive
pile of sand.

BUT...

...if I get covered
and my feet need to **wriggle**,
I poke out my toes and waggle them.

It makes my lizard **giggle!**

In my ocean,
there's a LOBSTER.

He's a **wiggly**, waving lobster, dip-diving through green water, claws snip-snapping— ready to **nip!**

I *swim, swim swim* away,
and ride
the **bubbly**
swirls.

BUT...

If he wants to dry himself
and *leaps* out of the bath...

I **splash** and **kick** the water
for a lovely lobster laugh.

On my mountain, there's a BEAR.
A hungry, **HAIRY** bear who jumps out
from nowhere, ready to eat me!

I *climb, climb, climb,*
as fast as I can.

BUT...

...if he saves me from a **fall**,
I hold on very tight...

...and tell him he's the best bear of all, and give him...